To Rescue My Princess

A Turnberry Legacy Short Story

~~~

Lane McFarland

Please visit Lane McFarland's website at

http://www.lanemcfarland.com/

to learn more about her and her books.
~~~

To Rescue My Princess

It's 1306, a turbulent time in Scotland. King Robert the Bruce is on the run, leaving his family and supporters vulnerable and exposed.

When English soldiers attack the Bruce's family, Morgana, one of the Scottish Queen's ladies, also is arrested and locked in an iron cage suspended over the side of Conwy Castle. Brutalized and humiliated at the hands of her enemies, she grasps a tenuous lifeline of revenge.

Alysander, a Scottish warrior, returns to Stonecrest to ask for Morgana's hand in marriage and learns of her capture. Determined to rescue her, he and his men undertake a dangerous mission to set her free.

Will Alysander succeed in rescuing Morgana from her barbarous imprisonment? Will love be enough to free her from her vehement desire for revenge?

TO RESCUE MY PRINCESS

Published by Amazon KDP

Seattle, WA

Electronic KDP Edition: September 2020

~~~

To Rescue My Princess is a work of fiction.
~~~

TABLE OF CONTENTS

Chapter One

St. Duthas Chapel
Tain, Scotland
September 1306

"Run!" Morgana clasped Marjorie's small hand and dashed up the grassy knoll with the four other women. Out of breath, they hurried through the cemetery's iron gate and hid behind cracked and crumbling headstones discolored by green lichen and mold.

The cacophony of clashing steel, the echoing throb of military drums, and the stamping feet of advancing soldiers reverberated through Morgana's ears. Her heart beat so fast, it near exploded.

The English made no attempt to hide their approach. In broad daylight, they marched forward with purpose to capture and arrest Robert the Bruce's relatives and supporters who had fled the slaughter at Kildrummy Castle last eve.

Images of soldiers dragging a battered Nigel Bruce into the bailey flashed through her mind. His brother, King Robert, had escaped the country with a small contingent after the Scots' crushing defeat at the Battle of Methven, leaving his family vulnerable and exposed.

She shuddered.

Blessed Nigel had distracted the troops long enough for his family, along with Isabella, Countess of Buchan, and Morgana, to escape.

She prayed he still lived.

"Where shall we go?" Queen Elizabeth cried. "What will we do?"

"We have to get to the Orkneys. To safety," Morgana stated. As one of the queen's ladies, she would do everything she could to protect the queen.

"There they are!" A shout rang out at the base of the hill.

Isabella stared down at the men, a look of horror etched on her face. "Dear heavens. They're upon us!"

A group of soldiers stormed toward the women.

Morgana held Marjorie's slender shoulders and steered the eleven-year-old to the queen. "Retreat up the hill and inside the chapel. I'll hold them off as long as I can."

The queen's brow furrowed as Marjorie ran into her arms. "Morgana, donnae risk yerself."

"The chapel is a place of sanctuary, and I'm praying ye will be safe there, my queen." Morgana looked to the others as she tugged her bow from her back and nocked an arrow. "All of ye, go now. Hurry!"

The women hastened away.

Morgana's pulse pounded in her head. She peered from behind the stone grave marker and concentrated on holding her aim steady on the gate's narrow opening.

I can do this. Just like hunting, except the prey will be racing toward me. I have but a moment to wait before I pick them off.

A soldier leading the charge appeared, his stare focused on the chapel.

Her stomach tightened. With a deep breath, she loosed her arrow. It struck him in the neck. The man grabbed the shaft and toppled to the ground.

She nocked another barb as the next soldier ran forward. One after another, she dispatched three more advancing troops as they slipped inside the gate. The soldiers fell back for cover, firing their own arrows her way. More and more troops stormed the hill.

She was outnumbered.

Chapter Two

Morgana hoisted her skirt and sprinted up the hill. Arrows whistled by her head. Others stuck in the ground near her racing feet. An arrow sliced her sleeve and grazed her skin. A burn coursed down her arm.

Lord, help me!

With one last burst of energy, she darted into the chapel. "Bar the door."

Two monks thrust a wooden beam through iron brackets, blocking the entrance.

Morgana hooked her bow over her shoulder and stepped back from the door. The chapel's fortifications were never intended to repel advancing soldiers. It was only a matter of time before the defenses no longer provided protection.

Whimpers sounded behind her and she turned to Isabella, huddled with the Bruce's sisters, Christina and Mary. Marjorie, the king's daughter, clung to the queen. Their widened eyes and dirt-streaked, ashen faces appeared stark in the dim light.

"Is there no way out through the back of the building?" Morgana asked the monks.

One shook his balding head. "No. 'Tis only this entryway."

Wham!

Morgana jumped.

The women shrieked.

The door held, but for how long?

Wham!

Splinters broke away with each strike.

Dear God!

Morgana's stomach twisted. Legs braced apart and arms shaking, she nocked another arrow and pointed it at the door. She'd die defending her queen and her friends.

With another strike, the wooden slats creaked apart, giving way to the onslaught. Chainmail-clad soldiers stormed into the chapel.

One of the monks ran forward, a large cross dangling from a chain around his neck, aged hands up as if to prevent the invasion. "This is a holy place of sanctuary," he cried. "Ye cannae come in here bearing arms."

"In the name of the king, get out of the way, old man." A burly fiend knocked the monk aside and led the troops farther into the sanctuary.

Hands on hips, he glared at Morgana, her arrow aimed at his chest.

"Ye heard the good brother," she snarled. "There's no need for drawn swords in a house of worship. This place is holy—a shrine—under the protection of the church."

"Permit me to introduce myself." A sneer distorted his pompous expression as he stepped forward.

She raised her bow higher, her eye trained on the man. "Come no closer."

He stopped and held up his hands. "You had best lower your weapon. You are surrounded."

A squeal rent the air behind her.

She spared a glance over her shoulder.

A soldier held a struggling Marjorie against his chest.

"Please, donnae hurt her," Queen Elizabeth wailed. "She's naught but a child."

Bile churned in Morgana's stomach.

"I'll not tell you again. Lower yer weapon, mistress, or it will not bode well for the girl."

Hopelessness spread through her like wildfire. Her legs trembled and she dropped her arm. A soldier rushed her, snatched the quiver of arrows from her back and the bow out of her hands.

The searing burn from the arrow that had grazed her skin earlier stung. Blood wet her hand as she rubbed the injury.

"I am the Earl of Ross, devoted to Comyn, the *rightful* King of Scotland. That is until he was murdered by Robert the Bruce." He marched over to her and squeezed her cheeks, lifting her to her toes.

She winced, her fingers trying to dislodge his agonizing grip.

"Where is the Bruce?" His hold tightened.

Pain shot through her face. "I donnae know."

"Tell me now."

"Threaten all ye want. It willnae change my answer. I donnae know where the Bruce is."

Ross growled and shoved her to one of his men. She stumbled back against a guard. The man grasped her upper arms with steely pressure.

Ross yanked the queen forward, holding her mere inches from his face. "Where is he?"

She closed her eyes briefly as she shook her head. "He dinnae tell us where he was going. We donnae know."

Ross pushed her away with a smirk and addressed his men. "Take them to Tweed to meet their fate."

The soldiers hustled the women and Marjorie out of the chapel and through the yard. The Bruce's injured and dying men lay scattered across the holy grounds. The smell of death hung thick in the air.

Morgana swallowed hard. A man prodded her back, forcing her downhill toward a covered wagon.

She climbed into the bed, reached down to Marjorie, and tugged her up. Once they were all in the cart, the soldiers shackled their ankles to a ring secured in the floor's board. The wagon lurched forward and bounced along the bumpy road. Frigid air swirled around her, and she shivered uncontrollably from the temperature and from the fear racking her body.

What will become of us?

Chapter Three

Morgana placed her arms around Christina's and Marjorie's shoulders and looked to Mary, then Queen Elizabeth and Isabella. "Come, let's slide together for warmth."

The group huddled against each other as the procession transported them south to Berwick on England's east coast. Mary and Christina cried softly. The queen stroked Marjorie's head, tears escaping down her cheeks.

"Dinnae fret. Stay strong, my queen." Morgana cast her gaze over the others and ran a hand down Isabella's arm. "My friends, ye are all verra important in the Bruce's household. That alone will stave off harsh treatments."

Her words sounded believable enough. She just wished she possessed the confidence her voice portrayed.

***

Once at Berwick, the shackled women were paraded through the muddy castle bailey, their chains clanking between their feet and hands. Men and women filled the area, shouting insults and throwing rotting food at the small procession.

Morgana did her best to square her shoulders and ignore the obscenities, but she heard every horrid wish for her torturous death. A putrid, blackened cabbage slammed into her head and she reeled. Slimy leaves slid from her hair onto her soiled gown.

A beefy soldier yanked the chain. The women fell to the ground.

The crowd cheered.

Horrible, hateful people.

Morgana clenched her jaw as she scrambled to her feet and helped Mary up, while Queen Elizabeth and Christina steadied Marjorie and Isabella. With another jerk of the chain, the guard led them up a raised platform in the lower bailey where they were forced to stand for all to see.

Morgana lifted her chin and glared at the loathsome horde.

Moments later, a guard yelled, "Nigel Bruce, brother to the murderous Robert the Bruce."

A horse galloped into the yard dragging a naked Nigel, his body blackened and swollen beyond recognition. The crowd roared with malice. Their barbarity had no bounds.

Morgana's heart lurched. She covered her mouth with her hand. Tears sprang to her eyes.

The commander ordered soldiers to cut him loose. They dragged him to an adjacent platform, threw a rope around his neck, and hoisted him high, legs kicking as the rope spun. The onlookers went wild. Cheers and shouts resounded through the bailey as Nigel twisted against the choking noose. All of a sudden, he dropped to the wooden platform, writhing, his face contorted and eyes bulging.

Queen Elizabeth held Marjorie's face against her middle, shielding the child from the horrendous brutality. The commander ordered his body quartered and the pieces sent across the countryside as *a gift* to the Bruce's supporters.

After Nigel's gruesome death, the commander turned his attention to the ladies as another stout man climbed the platform and faced the women.

He unrolled a parchment and read aloud. "It is the king's decree that Robert the Bruce's daughter, Marjorie, be sent to Gilbertine Convent at Watton. Robert's sister, Christina Bruce, to a convent in Lincolnshire. Robert's wife, Elizabeth de Burgh, will be placed under house arrest at a manor in Yorkshire."

"Nae, I willnae go without ye," Marjorie wailed, grasping Queen Elizabeth's waist.

"Shh," the queen whispered, large tears in her eyes. She stroked the child's back. "'Twill be a fine place for ye, my sweetling. Ye will be safe there."

The guard continued reading aloud. "Robert's sister, Mary Bruce, will be imprisoned in a wooden cage, exposed to public view at Roxburgh Castle."

A loud gasp filtered through the crowd. Mary bowed her head and clutched Christina's hand.

"The Countess of Buchan is to be imprisoned in a wooden cage, exposed to public view at Berwick Castle. And the queen's lady, Morgana McLeod, will be imprisoned in an iron cage, exposed to public view at Conwy Castle for an indefinite period of time."

Imprisoned in an iron cage at Conwy Castle. Dear Lord.

Morgana's stomach churned. Her knees wobbled and her legs almost collapsed. It took all her strength to stand before these people and show no reaction to their savagery.

The other women cried as soldiers pulled them apart and shuffled them off to their respective prisons.

A soldier seized Morgana's upper arm and jerked her forward. Tears blurred her eyes. She swiped a hand across her face and searched the crowd for the other ladies and wee Marjorie. Wails reached her ears, but she could not see the women through the swarm of spectators.

The man whisked her into a small iron-barred wagon. She fell on her side in the hard bed. He grabbed her leg and none too gently, clamped a cold metal shackle around her ankle and secured it to the floor.

He slammed the door and locked the cage with a clank.

She rose onto her knees and grasped the bars, peering out at the jeering crowd. Once again, Marjorie's cries reached her ears. Tears rolled down Morgana's cheeks as the cart lurched forward, starting the long journey to England's west coast.

The days and nights on the road melded into each other. She froze at night with little to no protection in the wagon. Bleakness spread through her upon realizing she'd be exposed to the elements in a cage like this for who knew how long.

An indefinite period of time.

Anguish threatened to engulf her. How would she survive? Winter fast approached.

She rubbed her forehead. *Collect yer wits. Donnae let them win. I cannae give them the satisfaction of my death.*

Someday, she would escape and seek revenge upon the Earl of Ross.

Focused on vengeance, determination sparked and flickered through her heart. She closed her eyes and grasped hold of the tenuous flame, her lifeline.

***

Once at Conwy Castle, the soldiers marched Morgana up the steep flight of stairs to the top of the castle. Wind whipped around her, tossing her long dark hair in her face and plastering her gown against her legs.

A guard holding a long spear led her to a square iron cage. Its door on top of the prison stood open, awaiting her.

A lump wedged in Morgana's throat and she struggled to breathe. The guard rushed her along, up a wooden ramp to the top of the cage.

"Get in."

She eased down to sit while dangling her legs inside the cage.

He pushed her shoulder, and she fell into the barred prison, landing hard on her knees. Pain shot up her legs and she rubbed the tender spots.

The guard slammed the door and removed the ramp. "Hoist her up," he shouted.

Two soldiers shoved a long crank. A loud grating noise screeched and the cage jostled from side to side.

She clutched the bars as the structure swung off the ground.

Another guard rotated a wooden beam to jut out over the side of the castle wall.

Morgana peered through the bars at her feet and gasped. The Conwy River's dark water smashed against boulders before rushing downstream.

She wrapped her arms about her legs and cried.

Dear Lord, give me strength.

***

The first few weeks were near unbearable. Autumn winds whistled off the water and swirled around her body clad in a filthy gown with only the protection of the thin blanket a good woman had tossed to her during a feeding. Once a day, the soldiers hoisted her up, and someone would open the lid and pass her food and water, only enough to sustain life. Then she remained on display.

She held up her chin at the taunting crowd, bearing humiliation, determined not to let them see her misery. The frigid nights sapped her strength, yet she prayed for a miracle—someone who'd save her from rotting in this wretched cage.

The cold bars matched the bleakness in her soul. Would Laird McLeod get word of her imprisonment? Would he come for her? What could he do to have her released?

Despair seeped into her veins, spreading dire tentacles of doom throughout her body. Many days and nights she thought she'd die—prayed she'd die and end this torture—but her dream of revenge kept her alive.

Alive for the day when she could witness the Earl of Ross take his last breath.

Chapter Four

Stonecrest Castle
South of Aberdeen
October 1306

Ocean spray peppered Alysander's face and cold wind cut through his heavy cloak as he sailed the *Dhìoghaltas* up the coast toward Laird Brandon McLeod's castle. The vessel sliced through the white-capped water with ease.

His body thrummed with anticipation as he rocked back on his heels. He let out a throaty laugh. After six long years, he was going to see Morgana again. He'd often thought of the dark-haired, blue-eyed lass and the sweet kiss she'd given him when he last saw her. He could not wait to lay eyes upon her angel face again.

His younger brother, Bryce, joined him at the helm. "'Tis been a long time since visiting Lady Elsbeth and Laird Brandon. We were but lads when we left."

"Aye, young lads with high hopes."

Memories surfaced of Laird McLeod saving Alysander and Bryce when the English murdered their loved ones and burned their family's village. Since that time, the brothers had trained to sail under Laird MacAndrew's direction. Now, Alysander commanded his own merchant ship and had made enough profits to build a fortress tucked away in the forest of Loch Linnhe on the west coast. He always knew someday he would return for Morgana and ask her to join him on his island.

That day had finally arrived.

A stab of doubt sliced into his chest, threatening to shatter his rapturous dream. He'd not had contact with her in a long time. Would he find her married or promised to another? Would she still have amorous feelings toward him?

He took a deep breath. 'Twas only one way to find out.

A mountainous boulder rose from the ocean and transformed into a daunting stone fortress. Gray clouds blocked the waning sun, cloaking the immense structure in eerie shadows. Golden flames from torches lining the battlements flared into the evening sky. Warriors patrolled ramparts between round bastions positioned at the castle's corners.

Stonecrest was just as he remembered.

Alysander moored his boat in the cove below the castle and headed up the hill on horseback with Bryce and two of his men following. The imposing gray structure soared above the sheer sea-cliff and raging ocean. The waves pummeled its foundation. Glowing torches revealed defensive arrow-slits positioned at strategic locations, and men armed with broadswords, bows, and arrows marched along the fortified battlements.

Snapping in the wind, Stonecrest's white banner graced with two elk waved over the castle. He studied the pennant. Raised on hind feet, the animals flanked a blue shield and a golden eagle presided above the elk. The symbols representing freedom, strength, independence, and pride characterized the laird's spirit, beliefs, and convictions.

The brothers owed the man their lives. In many ways, they were returning home.

Alysander was close to Stonecrest Castle—close to seeing Morgana again. He squeezed his legs around Cadarn's girth, and the horse broke into a full gallop. He laughed into the wind. Bryce and the others would have to keep pace.

Chapter Five

Roussel ushered Alysander, Bryce, and the others into the castle's great room where the laird's wife, Elsbeth, and adopted children, Alainne, Lena, and Bodwyn, sat before a blazing hearth. How the lad and lasses had grown.

The four jumped from their chairs and rushed toward them.

"Oh, Alysander and Bryce." Elsbeth hugged one, then the other. "We're so happy ye've come. Please have a seat."

Bryce dropped onto the bench beside Bodwyn, the two friends smiling and quickly catching up with each other.

Alysander turned to his men. "This is David and Bram. They sail with me."

"Welcome to our home." Elsbeth smiled warmly then clasped Alysander's hand. "'Tis verra good to have ye here. I so wish Brandon and Tristian knew of yer visit. They have gone to the Bruce's aid in Ireland and will be sorely disappointed to have missed ye."

Alysander exhaled loudly. "Mangus told me Brandon signed the *Turnberry Bond* and has been instrumental in helping the Bruce and the cause."

"After the Bruce's defeat at the Battle of Methven, that bond between the nobles and lairds is more important than ever. Our king needs all the support he can garner."

Roussel entered the room carrying a tray of tankards and sweetmeats. He passed the refreshments around.

"Thank ye." Alysander nodded at the man, took a swig of ale, then balanced the tankard on his thigh. "Laird MacAndrew recruited me in the fight against the English. King Edward is sending troops into Scotland to rout Bruce supporters. Ye need to be verra careful, Elsbeth. The *Dragon Banner* has been raised. If Edward were to get wind of what Brandon is doing, he would attack and kill all in his wake. He will grant no quarter."

She shuddered and briefly closed her eyes. "I understand and appreciate yer warning. I hope ye'll all take care as well."

He shrugged. "'Tis safe enough. We deliver food and supplies in ports along the coast for the warriors in hiding still fighting for the Bruce. The rebellion has suffered a devastating setback. We have to rebuild, restore the drive against Edward and his determination to rule Scotland and eradicate our way of life, our freedom."

"I agree. I only worry about our safety."

Alysander could barely stand a minute longer without seeing Morgana. He'd thought of this time so often over the years, wondered how she was getting along. She'd been three and ten summers when he'd last seen her—a budding young lass who captured his heart.

"'Tis been quite a while since I was here last." He glanced around the hall. "Is…is everyone well?"

Satan's toes! Why can't I just come out and ask about her?

Elsbeth ran a hand down Lena's arm. "Aye, we miss the men when they are gone, but we're managing."

Alainne bumped Elsbeth's elbow. "I think he's asking about Morgana."

Bright lass.

Elsbeth straightened. "Ye are here because of Morgana?"

"Aye…well, I also wanted to see ye and the laird, too." He smiled. "Will ye tell her I am here?"

Her eyes misted with tears.

Alysander tilted his head. "What is it? Why do ye cry?"

She held up a hand, then rubbed her forehead. "Of course, ye wouldnae have heard."

His chest tightened. "Heard what?"

She gazed at him with doleful eyes. "Morgana was with the Bruce's wife, Queen Elizabeth, when they fled

Kildrummy. She was arrested and is being held prisoner in Conwy Castle." She put a hand over her mouth and shook her head. More tears flowed down her face. "They imprisoned her in a cage over the side of the castle."

His heart pounded at a dizzying speed.

Arrested? Held prisoner in a cage?

Alainne rubbed Elsbeth's back as the lady pinched the skin at her throat. "I was uncertain as to whether to let her go with Queen Elizabeth's party last fall, but Morgana is a grown woman. I could not keep her here under my skirt forever." She tugged a linen square from inside her sleeve and wiped her eyes. "I should have forbidden her to leave, but she saw this as a grand opportunity, one she'd never have again."

Alysander stood and marched to the hearth. He paced back to her. "When? When did this happen?"

"Almost a month ago. I sent a missive to Brandon informing him of Morgana's arrest and the Bruce's family's imprisonment the moment I received the message last week, but I havenae heard from him yet."

"Dinnae fash." Alysander knelt before her and grasped her wringing hands. "I'm going after her. Let Brandon know. I'll send word of her safety as soon as I can."

"Oh, nae, Alysander. 'Tis too dangerous. Ye could be killed…or worse."

"My life wouldnae be worth a fig without her." He straightened and looked to Bryce and his men. "Let's ride."

"Wait." Elsbeth stepped before him and placed a hand on his chest. "I know ye must be tired. Will ye nae stay the night and leave in the morning after ye've rested?"

"I cannae rest until I know she is safe."

Elsbeth sighed with a nod. "I understand. And I thank ye."

She walked the men to the door, then clutched Alysander's arm and gazed into his eyes. "Morgana is nae a princess who might be leverage for Edward. He uses her as an example to other supporters without raising the Bruce's ire like he would should he mistreat Queen Elizabeth."

Alysander's stomach clenched.

Royal blood might not flow through Morgana's veins, but she was *his* princess, and he would do everything in his power to see her released. The lass had nothing to do with the war or the cause. She'd only been part of the court, serving her queen—her friend—Elizabeth, and by God, he would set Morgana free.

Chapter Six

Alysander and his men sailed around the northern tip of Scotland and down the coast to the Menai Strait. They hid the ship south of Conwy River and struck out on horseback.

After what seemed an agonizing eternity, Alysander led the riders into the village. An iron cage hung over the side of the castle.

Morgana sat within, huddled in a ball.

His body tensed and he clenched his fist around Cadarn's reins. Heat flushed through him at witnessing her suffer, but it appeared the villagers had all but forgotten her, as if it were commonplace to see a lass imprisoned in a cage. They bustled about the bailey, not even glancing up. That heinous attitude would serve him well this evening. Perhaps not being a Bruce family member would prove advantageous. No one expected an attempt to free her. The fortune of surprise was on his side.

After midnight, he and several of his men crept into the lower level of the castle off the river. The water splashed against the stone pillars, and a cold wind whipped around them. How could Morgana endure the perilous weather?

His heart hammered in his ears. He had to reach her straight away, end her torture.

He stealthily slipped up behind a guard and bashed the back of the soldier's head with his dirk's handle. The unconscious man fell into Alysander's arms, then slid to the ground in a slump. David and Bram quickly subdued two other guards.

David swiped an arm over his brow. "The oil bags are hung and the archers are in place."

"Wait for my signal before the bags are lit." Alysander looked to Bram. "Come with me."

The two quietly climbed the outer stone stairs. Another soldier warmed his hands by an open fire. Bram slinked around the wall behind him, whacked the man over the head, and eased his limp body to the floor.

Two others stood ahead, looking out over the water. The guards whirled, hand on their blades' hilts.

Alysander thrust his dirk into one of the men before the guard had a chance to unsheathe his sword. He dropped beside the guard Bram stabbed.

Alysander nodded to Bram. They eased to the north side of the castle and peered over the edge. The cage, about ten feet down, dangled over the water. He leaned closer to Bram and spoke low. "We cannae risk the noise of rotating the beam."

"How will we get to her?"

"I'll climb down and hoist her up to ye."

Bram waited while Alysander inched along the wooden beam then down the chain holding the cage. It jostled under his weight, but his feet finally landed on the solid iron lid.

This must be how they feed her.

The top wasn't even locked. He eased the door open and peered down into Morgana's wide-eyed face.

"Lass, donnae be afraid. 'Tis me, Alysander." He held out a hand to her. "I'm getting ye out of here."

She crept closer. The cage rocked again, and she grasped the bars. "Alysander?"

"Aye, take my hand."

She reached for him. He grasped her small wrist and tugged her upward into his arms, steadying her on the swinging cage.

"Oh, my Lord," she cried against his chest. "I cannae believe ye are here."

He wanted to hold her, but now was not the time. "I need ye to climb up my body as high as ye can."

"What?" Panic laced her voice.

Alysander bent his right leg and clutched her elbow. "Step onto my thigh. My man will help ye up from above."

She wobbled as he eased her onto his leg.

"Grab the chain, lass."

She grasped it with both hands.

"Now, pull yerself up as I push ye. Bram will grab ye. He willnae let ye fall."

Alysander braced his feet apart then leaned against the iron line supporting the cage. Cupping his hands around her foot, he lifted her. The cage rattled, but she scrambled up the rusty chain.

"Gimme yer hand, mistress." Bram drew her up to straddle the wooden beam. "Donnae look down. Keep yer eyes fixed on me."

He inched across the beam with her.

She wobbled and gasped.

"Easy, jes a wee bit farther."

Alysander looked around them. All was quiet. He glanced back up as Bram tugged her onto the castle wall.

Hand over hand, Alysander clambered up the chain, then hoisted himself up and over the side. He drew her to him and rubbed her slender arms. God, she felt good, but she was verra thin. Dark circles marred the skin beneath her eyes, and her hollowed cheeks pronounced strong cheekbones.

"Halt!"

Chapter Seven

Alysander and Bram whirled, unsheathing their swords to face approaching English soldiers.

As the men charged, Alysander pushed Morgana to the side.

One of the soldiers swung his sword at Alysander's head.

Alysander darted back.

The man lunged, his thrusts wild.

Clashing steel rang loud in the quiet night. A rush of strength born from the abuse meted out to Morgana surged through Alysander. This fiend would pay for what the English had done to her.

He slammed his blade against the soldier's chest. Vibrations rippled down his arm but he swung his sword with a vengeance and knocked the cur's weapon from his hands.

The soldier's sword clattered to the ground. He fell backward and landed hard. Hatred filled Alysander as he sank his blade deep into the man's gut.

Bram dispatched the other man, but not before he shouted a warning.

Stomping boots hitting the rough pavers resounded against the castle walls.

"Now, David," Alysander yelled. "Now!"

Blazing arrows flew from the darkness at the advancing soldiers as he grabbed Morgana's hand. Joined by Bram, the three dashed down the stone steps to the lower level.

The river rushed before them. Running soldiers' pounding boots echoed in the corridor to the left. More sounded from the right. The escape route was cut off.

Shite!

They'd have to jump. Did Morgana have the strength to make it to shore? *Hell!* They had no choice.

"Are ye well enough for a swim, lass? I fear 'tis the only way out."

***

"I would do *anything* to escape that cage." Morgana took a deep breath and jumped into the river. Freezing water engulfed her, roared in her ears.

Dear Lord!

Arms flailing, she broke the surface and gasped for air.

Her body trembled uncontrollably.

A swift current carried her downstream.

Where's Alysander?

She looked right then left, but couldn't discern shapes in the darkness.

Flaming arrows flew over her head and rained upon the castle's soldiers. A loud explosion rent the air behind her.

She jerked, her heart pounding.

Fire lit the dark night.

"Dinnae fash." Alysander swam up beside her. "'Tis my men providing cover from shore."

Bram appeared next to them. "That should keep them busy."

"Aye, but not for long. We must hurry," Alysander urged.

A wave of dizziness washed over Morgana. She blinked, trying to focus. She attempted to swim across the current toward the riverbank, but her arms and legs moved as if mired in quicksand.

Water splashed her face.

Her breathing sped up, teeth chattering.

"I donnae…I donnae know if I can make it." She coughed, choking. "I cannae seem to move."

"'Tis the cold, lass. I'll help ye." Alysander turned her back to his chest, grasped her beneath her arms, and kicked, propelling them toward the shore. "Keep moving yer legs." He gurgled water. "Kick with me if ye can."

Finally, they reached land. Men rushed into the water. One lifted her from Alysander, carried her ashore, and set her feet on the muddy bank.

"The archers will meet us at the ship," the man said.

Alysander emerged from the river, water pouring off his clothes as he marched onto the beach. "Verra guid." Breathing hard, he clasped her hand. "We must go!"

They strode toward his horse. Her legs weakened, and she stumbled. Her other hand shot out to break the fall, but Alysander tugged her up before her knees hit the ground. He lifted her into his arms. She clung to him as he broke into a run.

The horse tossed his head as Alysander hoisted her up and onto the animal's back behind the saddle. She grabbed hold of the leather and settled her legs on either side of the rounded back.

Alysander leapt up in front of her. "Hold on, princess."

She hugged his muscular body, molding herself against his wet back. Nothing had ever felt so good.

The horse galloped away, his men thundering behind. Shouts from the castle rang through the night, and a deafening knell clanged from the bell tower.

Morgana briefly closed her eyes.

Please, God, see us safely away.

Chapter Eight

Shivers from cold and fear coursed through Morgana. Her teeth rattled. The sennights she'd spent crammed in that dreadful cage had sapped the strength from her muscles, but she held onto Alysander with all her might.

After six long years, he is really here.

Stories of his daring adventures at sea, how he commanded his ship and outwitted the enemy while aiding the Bruce, had reached her at Stonecrest. She'd always listened with keen interest to visitors when his name was mentioned.

As an orphaned lass of three and ten, she'd regarded him as a hero. He'd shown her kindness and comforted her when she relived nightmares about the night of her family's slaughter. Over the years, she'd begun to think her reverence was no more than adoration for a braw, older lad. She convinced herself he'd not return as he'd promised, for surely his words were simply to mollify a young lass.

Yet here he is.

Her heart swelled and she hugged him tighter.

The horses raced along a worn path bordering the river's shoreline, their hooves muffled by a thick layer of damp autumn leaves. After some time, Alysander slowed the animal to a trot and entered a clearing beside the water's edge.

The sliver of moon highlighted a ship hidden in a cove off the bay.

Her shoulders eased. What a wondrous sight.

Men ran across the deck and down the plank toward them. The main sail was hoisted, and wind filled the unfurling canvas. Other crewmen dashed along the railing, pulling ropes and securing lines.

Alysander reined in the horse.

An older man raced forward and gripped the reins. "Bryce has the ship readied."

Alysander jumped to the ground. "Bring the horses on board and let's get underway."

"Aye, sir."

Morgana eased into Alysander's arms and he lowered her beside him.

Her legs buckled and she nearly collapsed. "Heavens, I'm so weak."

"Given a wee bit of time, ye'll regain yer strength." He placed an arm around her back and the other beneath her legs then carried her toward the ship. "Once ye warm, ye'll feel more like yerself."

With her arms around his neck, Morgana rested her head on his chest.

She was exhausted.

And cold.

And hungry.

But she couldn't be happier. Her love had rescued her from a horrific fate. She'd die before she'd return to that cage.

Chapter Nine

Alysander strode across the worn plank and dropped to the deck with Morgana cradled in his arms.

Bryce stopped beside them and took her hand. "Morgana, 'tis so verra guid to see ye."

"And ye, Bryce." He'd grown into such a tall, strapping man, much like his older brother.

"I must take her below. Get us out to sea quickly."

"Right away." Bryce hurried off.

"Ye may put me down. I can manage from here," Morgana fretted. Alysander needed to be on deck, commanding his men. "I donnae want to be any more of a bother."

"Ye'll never be a bother."

He navigated the creaking steps to below deck. Hammocks filling the area swayed in the gentle waves. His damp shoulder-length hair slid over her arm as he weaved between the men's quarters, through an open door, and into a small cabin. He placed her on a cot, then grasped the mattress when the ship rocked.

"Guid. We're underway, headed out to sea."

Her heart lightened. She rubbed the chill-bumps on her arms. "Everything happened so fast. I cannae believe I'm really free."

"Aye, well, we arenae out of danger yet, but the farther we travel tonight, the better." He knelt beside a chest at the foot of his cot and rummaged through the contents. "I know ye're cold in yer wet gown. We donnae have a bathing tub on board, but I do have a bucket of fresh water on the floor to yer right, a bowl and pitcher on the table, and here's a chunk of wood-ash that might help ye feel better."

Her heart melted over his concern for her comfort.

He set the brownish-colored wedge on the table beside the basin. Even with his head bent, his thick dark hair fell in waves to his broad shoulders.

"I also have a clean pair of trews and a tunic ye can wear until we find ye more suitable garments." He straightened and placed the clothing and a drying cloth on the side table. "Rest. I'll bring ye something to eat as soon as I can."

"I cannae thank ye enough."

A smile reached his ice-blue eyes, and he bowed slightly. "Ye're welcome. If ye'll excuse me, I'm needed on deck."

"Certainly. I understand."

He tipped his head to her, slipped out of the space, and pulled the door closed.

She gazed around the cozy cabin. More chill-bumps dotted her skin, and she shivered. The pitcher and bowl sat beside a flask and cups on the table, along with maps and strange-looking instruments. A fair-sized chair was positioned to the side.

She rubbed the pounding in her head and inhaled deeply. Her body shook from the cold. She needed to get out of these wet clothes before she froze to death. It would be heavenly to scrub off the dirt and grime she'd suffered then don the clean, dry garments.

She eased off the cot and grasped the edge as she stood, her legs trembling as if she were a newborn bairn. *Gracious.* The time spent confined left her body spent. She spied the wooden bucket then shuffled over to it, placed it beside the table, and dipped the pitcher into the cold water.

The ship listed to one side then the other, but she was determined to rid herself of the filth caked on her skin—filth from that horrible prison.

She stripped out of her nasty clothes, poured water in the basin, and scrubbed her pinking skin. Her ribs and hip bones protruded. With little to eat, she'd lost weight. She ran a hand over a hollowed cheek and down her neck.

She must look a fright. When she'd dreamed of Alysander's return, she envisioned greeting him dressed in her favorite gown, her hair styled.

He has certainly seen me at my worst.

After drying off, she slipped into the trews and shirt he left on the table. His woodsy scent filled her nose. She wrapped her arms around herself and thanked God for sending him to her. She prayed they would make it out of here safely.

King Edward's men were no doubt on their trail.

Chapter Ten

A cold wind blew across the Irish Sea, greeting the Dhìoghaltas as she glided through choppy waves. Muscles tight, Alysander stepped from the helm and stretched his neck to the right, then left. It had been a long two days, but he and his men had successfully plucked Morgana from King Edward's stronghold, and the ship was well into her voyage to Loch Linnhe.

He didn't fool himself into thinking her rescue was so simple, that it was over. The English monarch would be furious someone extracted his prisoner from beneath his soldiers' noses and would be relentless in pursuit of her.

Alysander couldn't run the risk of returning her to Stonecrest. Not that he was unhappy about that conclusion. It provided another reason to escort her to his island, show her his home, and help her realize the merits of staying with him and building a life together.

Carlton strode across the deck and stepped before him. "I'll take her for ye, Chief. 'Tis time for my watch."

"Hold her steady to the west of Man."

"Aye, sir."

"Bryce will relieve ye before long." Alysander tugged his cloak tighter about his neck and made his way down the stairs. He weaved between swinging cots filled with snoring men and strode into his cabin, pulling the door closed behind him.

Curled on her side, Morgana was fast asleep on his cot. He shrugged off his wet cloak and hung it on a nail in the post beside the door. A chill swept around him as he shuffled through his trunk, pulling out a shirt and a pair of trews.

Stripping down nude, he watched the lass. She slept soundly. He shoved his legs into the trews and tossed the shirt over his head. The dry clothing felt good against his cold skin. The unexpected swim in the freezing river had chilled him to the bone.

He grabbed the wineskin as he sat in the chair, then gulped a mouthful. Blissful heat spread through his chest to his stomach. Another swig and he stuffed the wax stopper back into the spout.

Dark hair framed Morgana's soft face, marred with shadows and thinned from her prolonged hunger and insufferable imprisonment. His garments swallowed her small frame. Her delicate hand rested on the mattress, and her long tresses fanned out behind her.

How he'd missed her.

He'd thought of her so often, but never envisioned their reunion to take place while rescuing her from an abominable prison.

Morgana had suffered terribly recovering from the murder of her family, much like what happened to his own clan. Now she faced getting past her imprisonment in that cage. He vowed to lavish her with love, help her heal, and move past the horrific time spent at Conwy Castle, alone and frightened, cold and hungry. He would protect her. Never let her suffer such brutality again.

She whimpered and her brow furrowed.

He set his wineskin on the table, laid down behind her, and tugged her to him. "Shh…*mo chroí*. Ye are safe. I willnae let anyone harm ye."

She quieted and snuggled against him.

He closed his eyes and relished the feel of her in his arms.

"Once again ye've helped me through a nightmare. I've not forgotten yer comfort years ago."

He stroked her arm with a thumb. "Ye've had a rough go of it for a long time."

The ship rocked. The wood creaked and groaned in the swells.

"I began to lose hope I'd ever be free," she whispered. "I thought I'd die in that cage."

"I am sorry ye were caught up in Edward's savagery. I wish I had been able to save ye from experiencing his barbarity."

She glanced at him over her shoulder. "Ye did save me, Alysander. I will be forever grateful."

Chapter Eleven

The afternoon sun sat low on the horizon as Alysander steered the ship northeast toward the Inner Hebrides. Orange and red swathes painted the deep blue sky, the colorful reflection shimmering across the windswept cove. The ship glided through the calm water as if eager to put into port. Soon they would reach his island. After the months he and his men had spent sailing the shores of France, Spain, and Ireland, he looked forward to arriving and, hopefully, settling Morgana in his home.

"Good evening."

He turned as she stepped up behind him.

"I'm glad to see ye up and about."

She pulled a blanket around her shoulders. "I slept like I was dead."

"'Tis guid ye rested. Ye'll need more sleep along with nourishing food to regain yer strength."

"Aye, I still feel tired." She leaned a hip against the railing, her dark hair whipping in the wind. She captured the thick strands in her hand and pulled them before her while staring ahead.

"Ye've been through a terrible ordeal. 'Twill take time to heal both body and soul."

A thoughtful expression passed over her face. "How did ye know I was imprisoned?"

"Elsbeth told me. I had sailed to Stonecrest to…to see ye."

She looked at him, her eyes widened. "Ye did?"

"I told ye I would come back for ye." He cupped her cheek. "I've thought of ye day and night."

The smile she gave him brightened her blue eyes. "Oh, Alysander, I have longed to hear ye say those words."

She stepped into his embrace and wrapped her arms around his waist. He rested his chin on top of her head.

They held each other for a while without speaking, swaying in the gentle waves of Loch Linnhe.

He rubbed her back then straightened and clutched her shoulders. "I'm taking ye to my home on an isle in the Inner Hebrides. Ye remember Laird Mangus MacAndrew? His family has owned the island for many generations. The land was uninhabited—a guid spot where I've found safe harbor."

"Safe harbor?"

"I transport food and supplies to the Bruce's supporters. For the most part, 'tis simply a matter of making a delivery and sailing on, but there've been occasions when 'twas prudent to stay hidden for a time. The island is unknown to most and provides refuge for my men, their families, Bryce, and me."

"I see." She gazed at him. "I remember Laird MacAndrew with fondness. He visited Stonecrest several times and was always indulgent of my questions about ye and yer sailing adventures. He said ye were quite busy, supporting the Bruce and working hard for the cause."

She'd asked about me. Alysander's chest swelled.

"Ahh, well, I'm taking a wee break. We're just now returning from months of sailing, and I aim to stay put for a while. Ye'll be safe hidden there. With the Dragon Banner raised, King Edward has his son leading troops into Scotland to uncover supporters who aid the Bruce. They lay siege to any and all who are deemed suspicious. We must be careful."

"Have ye heard anything about the queen, Marjorie, and the other ladies from Kildrummy Castle?"

"They're still imprisoned. I'm sure the Bruce will send men to their rescue. Once we have ye safely on the island, I'll see what I can find out about their plight."

She glanced down and fidgeted with the string on the trews. "I appreciate yer offer to protect me, but I ask ye take me to Tain."

"Tain? Why?"

"Revenge."

He knew that feeling all too well.

Water lapped against the hull. Ropes creaked and chains rattled on the tall mast as the ship glided farther up the loch.

Her eyes glinted. "Knowing someday I'd reap vengeance upon Ross's head kept me alive."

"Ye donnae want his death on yer hands, lass."

"Aye, I do. Ye donnae know how much I want that man dead for what he did to us, for what his kind did to Nigel Bruce." A tear slid down her cheek, and her hands fisted. "I've never before witnessed nor endured such savagery."

He tugged her to him again and held her. Her slender shoulders shook as she let go of pent-up emotion. Soon she sagged against him, her body spent.

"I know yer pain. I, too, have been intent on avenging my family. Hell, I even named this ship after my determination, but ye are much too weak to undertake such a task."

She straightened and looked at him with teary eyes. "I am weak, but I will strengthen and when I do, I will have my vengeance."

"Ye must wait, bide yer time, and form a plan."

"Ye will help me with such a plan?"

He kissed her forehead. "I will."

Chapter Twelve

The Inner Hebrides stretched out before Morgana, the multitude of islands dotting Scotland's west coast. Two white-tailed sea eagles soared above the rocky mountain range, their high-pitched calls echoing across steep snow-covered hills towering in the distance.

The Dhìoghaltas eased through the placid loch around a stand of dense evergreens. Morgana stood at the ship's railing and inhaled deeply. She would soon meet all of Alysander's people. How she wished she could repay them for the risk they'd undertaken in rescuing her. If King Edward learned of their part in her escape, the inhabitants would pay dearly.

'Twas another reason for her to leave as soon as she was able. She would not add to the danger these good people had already incurred. Too many had suffered. Too many had died.

Alysander guided the ship into a cove surrounded by a wide beach. Torches raised on poles positioned around the forest's border provided wavering light across a long pier jutting into the inlet. Several men holding thick ropes jumped from the ship to the wooden structure and slowed the vessel. The side scraped the bulwark, the wood screeching as the crew brought the Dhìoghaltas to rest.

Women ran onto the beach to greet husbands, sons, and brothers. Laughter and squeals filled the air. Several lasses racing by hugged Alysander as he walked hand-in-hand with Morgana up the trail to the village. A dirt path wide enough for a wagon wound through the forest to a clearing. A stout wooden barn with open doors sat to the left. A wagon wheel and numerous round barrels rested against the walls of the two-story structure.

A short way beyond, thatched-roofed houses lined the dirt road. A mill and pasture of grazing sheep and goats were on the other side of a fast-moving stream. Several men worked in the field, and a lady carrying a basket strolled by and waved.

"Good evening to ye, Chief," she said. "Welcome home."

Alysander tipped his head to her. "Thank ye, Glenda. 'Tis guid to be back."

They continued uphill as he pointed out the different structures, explaining who lived where and the role they played in the group. They made their way to a fine three-story wooden home.

"This is my manor."

He placed a hand at the small of her back and guided her into a large great room filled with tables and benches and graced by a wide hearth on the back wall. Two young lads stoked a fire while roasting a slab of meat over the flames. The aroma filled her senses and her stomach growled. She would cherish a wee taste of the scrumptious smelling meat.

"We are a small but close community. The women use the cookhouse to prepare meals, and everyone gathers in this common chamber to eat, visit, and air grievances when warranted."

The ladies cheerfully prepared for a celebration of the return of their men and her successful rescue as Alysander showed her around and introduced her to the others. Their friendly smiles and kind welcomes warmed her heart. Two of the women pampered her with a hot bath, a fresh gown, and clean underthings.

Heat radiated through her chest. She never expected such a heartfelt reception. *What wonderful people.*

Smoked salmon, roasted boar, and tankards of wine and mead lined the trestle tables. Women and men danced to the lively harmonicas and lutes played by ale-drinking, merry-making lads. Cheers and laughter rang throughout the great hall. As the hour grew late, the music slowed, and couples slowly drifted onto the dance floor.

Morgana strolled toward Alysander, who sat at a table amongst his men. She extended a hand. "Do ye care to dance?"

He placed his tankard on the table and accepted her invitation.

A fluttering started in her stomach at the simple touch of his hand in hers. She smiled as they bowed to each other, stepped close then slid away. They rotated around, placed their hands together, and once again stepped close.

He gazed down at her, and she tipped her head up to him—her heart pounding. He placed his mouth on hers, and she closed her eyes, inhaling his musky scent. He trailed his lips along her cheek to nibble on her ear. Tingles shot through her and her legs grew weak.

***

Upon seeing Morgana again, now as a grown woman, Alysander realized his feelings grew stronger than he'd imagined possible. Aye, he remembered the young lass he'd fallen in love with. He thought of her so often, praying she awaited his return and that she too would want him as he wanted her.

"Come walk the shore with me," he whispered in her ear. "I want to speak with ye…alone."

She straightened and gazed into his eyes. "Verra well."

He led her down to the water's edge. The crescent moon sent glimmers along the rippling surface.

"'Tis beautiful," she said on a breath.

Alysander stepped behind her and wrapped his arms around her. "Aye, 'tis a sight I donnae tire of seeing."

The water lapped on shore, and a gentle breeze blew around them.

"Ye said ye wanted to talk to me. Is it about helping me with my plan?"

"Aye. There are many forms of revenge, lass, and I want to help ye plan the sweetest vengeance."

"I'm listening."

"The best reprisal by far is ye succeeding, being happy, and living a good life, regardless of what the fiend did to ye. I implore ye, take that kind of vengeance."

She stiffened. "I donnae know if that would be enough to heal my heart, stifle my anger, my pain."

He hugged her tighter. "There are many here who have been wronged, myself included. For years, I held onto the vow of retaliation, but it seared a black mark on my soul, one that spread through my core."

A splash sounded in the cove and then another as seals frolicked in the cool night. Morgana remained quiet and still in his arms.

"I like to think I bested the English dogs," he continued. "Bryce and I survived their brutal attack. Aye, we lost loved ones, but we werenae defeated. Through new friends and family, we have thrived in spite of our enemy. They dinnae win."

Still she said nothing.

Alysander turned her toward him. He searched her face, her eyes. "Say something."

She shook her head. "I have to go back. I have to get revenge."

"You could be killed."

"It doesnae matter."

"Aye, it does. It matters to me."

Morgana stared into his eyes.

"I understand yer anger and pain, but revenge keeps yer anguish alive. It eats away at yer soul. Ye have to release yer desire to kill the man. Embrace the good in yer life. 'Tis nae to say ye willnae think on it a time or two, and maybe someday circumstances will arise when ye can easily deliver a blow to yer enemy without causing harm to yerself, but donnae dwell on it. Donnae let him win by destroying yer happiness and replacing it with darkness and grief."

"I still see his sneer, hear his order to take us away. Marjorie's screams and Elizabeth's cries fill my ears."

"Ye will for some time but 'twill fade." He gazed at her, his heart bared. "Choose me, Morgana. Nae the revenge."

***

She rubbed her forehead. If she sought Ross's death, Alysander would feel he had to go with her. Her chest tightened. If he died helping her kill the man, she would never forgive herself. So many had already lost their lives.

He took her hand in his. "Stay with me as my wife. Let us build a life together. I promise to lavish ye with love and give ye all the time ye need to heal, if ye'll stay."

Morgana's heart filled. God more than answered her prayers, her pleas from the torturous steel cage.

He sent her hero.

She'd loved Alysander since she met him so many years ago. He was still her champion.

"I donnae know what I did to deserve ye." She kissed his bearded cheek. "If ye managed to get past the horrors ye've endured, I will do my best to follow suit."

"Does that mean ye'll be my wife?"

She eased her arms around his neck and drew him in, placed her lips on his. "Aye, I will be yer wife, my love, forevermore."

Author's Note

Thank you for reading *To Rescue My Princess*. I hope you enjoyed it as much as I enjoyed writing it.

~~~

The Turnberry Legacy Series

To Support A King, the first book in *The Turnberry Legacy* series.

Plagued by atrocities he committed against innocent victims while pursuing his father's killers, Laird Mangus MacAndrew pledged to defend and provide for his clan. But his leadership is tested when two of his ships are attacked and his crews massacred. Desperate to fulfill his obligation to protect the clan, Mangus agrees to help reinstate *The Turnberry Bond*. His mission—garner support for the Bruce and avenge the deaths of his men.

The MacAndrew clan provides Catriona Butler something her Irish home could not, a safe haven. But when she receives a missive her brother is imprisoned and will be executed unless acceptable éraic can be obtained, she must return to her homeland.

Mangus agrees to take Catriona to Ireland and vows she will not become a distraction, but he longs to be near her. Catriona witnesses Mangus's fierce anger and grows distrustful. After a life of suffering her father's vicious temper, she is skeptical of anyone with a penchant for violence. She attempts to keep her distance, but her traitorous heart pulls her in Mangus's direction.

With the fate of the kingdom on his shoulders, will Mangus
~~~

reunite the men of *The Turnberry Bond*? Can he pursue vengeance against his enemies without taking more innocent lives? And can Catriona free her brother and grow to trust Mangus, staying true to her heart?

A King's Enemies, the second book in *The Turnberry Legacy* series.

Tormented by King Edward's brutality against Scottish sympathizers, Drake Fletcher vows revenge, but only a madman single-handedly attacks the Crown. Instead, he enters the royal court as a spy to aid Robert the Bruce's rise to power and place a formidable leader on Scotland's throne.

Scottish lass Katherine Mackenzie Armstrong targets three of King Edward's officers who brutally raped and murdered her mother. Disguised as one of Queen Margaret's attendants, she sets a course to destroy the men.

The acts of treason both Drake and Katherine commit are punishable by death in The Tower of London but their determination pushes dangerous limits. Considered enemies, they use each other to gain vital information. Neither expect their overwhelming attraction to one another, the staggering emotions stirred. But the closer they become, the more they jeopardize their pledges of vengeance.

Will the weight of retaliation crush them, see them beheaded? Or will Katherine and Drake form an alliance and learn to live and love again?

~~~
~~~

<u>*Death of a King's Rival*</u>, the third book in *The Turnberry Legacy* series.

Wracked with guilt over his absence when his father's clan was slaughtered by King Edward, Broden McClure vows to live a solitary life deep in a forest south of Dumfries, but when he is recruited to support the *Turnberry Bond*, he is thrown into a deadly clash between Robert the Bruce and the Red Comyn.

Naida Wolfe witnesses Robert the Bruce murder the Red Comyn. After hearing the order to eliminate any who might bear witness to the killing, Broden spies Naida hiding in an alcove and whisks her away, but not before they are spotted by the Bruce himself. Now branded a traitor for helping the lass, Broden escapes with Naida and they run for their lives.

When Naida learns Broden is the son of her clan's laird, she is furious to find he has lived all these years close by, forsaking the survivors of King Edward's attack, but she has no choice other than to flee with him to his grandfather's castle in Skye where she'll be safe. Both the Bruce's men and Comyn's are in pursuit. The Comyns want her to testify against the Bruce. The Bruce wants her dead.

Broden and Naida fight their growing attraction as they endure perilous escapades and the predicament thrust upon them while relying on each other for their very survival.

Will she be able to forgive Broden for abandoning her and the other survivors? Can Broden atone for his misgivings, earn Naida's trust, and get her to safety before the pursuers catch them?

~~~

Also, check out my other medieval Scotland series, ***The Daughters of Alastair MacDougall***.

The Daughters of Alastair MacDougall

Set in late thirteenth century Scotland, this series tells the stories of Laird Alastair MacDougall's four independent and oftentimes, headstrong daughters coming of age in a country fraught with war and feuds amongst rival clans. Follow his daughters as their lives become intertwined with four fierce, rebel highland warriors bent on eradicating the English soldiers from their homeland.

Cameron

Determined to band Scots together against English tyranny, Laird Robert Graham seals a truce with his feuding neighbor, the MacDougalls. But after his brother is nearly killed in a treacherous attack, Graham kidnaps the laird's daughter in an act of revenge.

Cameron MacDougall has devoted her life to the healing arts. She's long rebelled against her father's feuding ways, but when Robert Graham abducts her, she's finds herself at the center of the dispute between their families. She expects the anger she feels, not the simmering attraction to the powerful warrior, or the love she develops for his clan.
~~~

Can she stop further violence between the clans with her escape? Or will she find her surrender leads to a lasting peace and her own heart's desire?

Heather

Bent on overcoming the belief he's failed his aging father, Laird Alec Campbell concentrates on proving his worth to his people. He provides for them and leads men into battle, vowing never again to disappoint his clan or lose his heart.

Bound by a promise to her dying mother, Heather MacDougall secretly leads rebel warriors in her quest to keep her clan intact and hold off those who plot to overtake her father's land. She fights to keep her secrets safe, while resisting the lure of the handsome young laird who challenges her defenses.

They can't deny their passionate attraction, but can their love survive their secrets?

Lindsey

Who said life was fair? Certainly not Lindsey MacDougall. She rebels at a world dominated by men. Dressed in lad's clothing, she manages her father's stables, caring for, breeding and selling horses. Unwavering on performing her duty to the rebellion, Lindsey throws caution to the wind and secretly delivers missives behind enemy lines to the Scottish warriors.

Logan Ross uses his happy-go-lucky smile to warm the hearts of many willing lasses, but it also masks his pain— the pain of his birth. As a bastard son, he is unacceptable for any Laird's daughter, including the spirited Lindsey MacDougall. However, she haunts his dreams. Determined to prove his worth, he throws himself into the middle of the rebellion, leading men into mortal danger.

After helping Logan escape from a brutal English dungeon, Lindsey fights her traitorous attraction to the virile highland warrior, vowing never to lose her heart to any man.

Elsbeth

Elsbeth MacDougall recoils at the violent Scottish rebellion and the bleak plight of orphans. Vowing to protect the homeless, she embarks on a journey to Scone and sets her course to become a nun, sheltering children from the cruelties of war. But when Brandon McLeod arrives at the Abby, he shakes her convictions and stirs provoking emotions she buried long ago.

After English soldiers murder his family, Brandon McLeod determines a course of revenge and leads numerous clans in Scotland's fight for freedom. Bent on the annihilation of English oppression, he is resolved to a life of solitude, vowing never to marry and chance the pain of losing loved ones again. However, that was before he met the enchanting Elsbeth.

~~~

A Medieval Christmas Novella

Morna MacAndrew yearns for her kindred spirit in a man, one she could cherish, and a wee bairn of her own. During a Scottish Yuletide holiday with family and friends, she discovers the man of her dreams. Her hopes are shattered when her brother, Laird Magnus MacAndrew, forbids their union. Her alliance-seeking brother would bend her to his
~~~

will and attach her to a man she does not love to provide a strategic alliance for the good of her clan and for all of Scotland during a turbulent time.

Kendrick Douglas, a seasoned warrior and would-be laird, on his way back to his clan after many years apart, finds a woman unlike all others, one that stirs his heart. But, because of Kendrick's qualms about one day being laird, Morna's brother is unaware of his lofty standing and is unable to see the possibilities their marriage could bring.

Can they convince Laird MacAndrew to let them follow their hearts?

~~~

To Love An Impostor

Consumed with hatred, Captain Nicholas Randolf Barlow pledges revenge against Bristol's gentry for the cruelty they inflicted on him and his friends when they were young orphans struggling to survive on the cruel city streets. Disguised as Nicholas Barlow, a ruthless, old businessman during the day, the Flintlock Brigand's leader at night, and Captain Randolf, in between, Nicholas works above suspicion to abscond with the gentry's possessions and to legally ruin the constables who failed to show the orphans mercy when they needed it most.

For the past twelve years, Diana Fleming, daughter of one of Bristol's wealthiest gentry, lived a simple, yet happy life in a small abbey far away from the bustling city. Her father
~~~

who was wracked with grief when her mother died, could not bear to be reminded of his loss, and sent his only daughter away to live in solitude. Diana, not willing to fade away quietly, finds comfort and purpose in tending the orphans of the abbey. When the small sanctuary is ordered to close, Diana returns to Bristol to beg her father for help with the raising of her ten orphan children, but instead discovers that her father died because of Nicholas Barlow. Now penniless and desperate, she's determined to destroy the man who murdered her father.

Nicholas's archenemy's daughter impresses him with her bartering skills and convinces him to rent her one of his homes. When he learns that she intends to raise a group of orphans on her own, his heart softens. As the Flintlock Brigand's leader he delivers much needed supplies to her at night. During the day, Captain Randolf helps her with the children. If she discovers that all three men are really the same man—the one she blames for her father's death—she will loath him for all eternity.

Can Nicholas forgo his vengeance and be truthful to Diana about his identity? Will Diana be able to forgive him, or will she hate him forever?

~~~

I would love to hear from you.

You can find me on Facebook at
https://www.facebook.com/LaneMcFarlandAuthor.
~~~

Please email me at mcfarland.lane@gmail.com and visit http://lanemcfarland.com to learn more about me and my books.